THE HAUNTED MUSTACHE

NIGHT FRIGHTS

BY **JOE McGEE**

ILLUSTRATED BY **TEO SKAFFA**

#1
THE HAUNTED MUSTACHE

ALADDIN

New York   London   Toronto   Sydney   New Delhi

This book is a work of fiction. Any references to historical events, real people, or real places are used fictitiously. Other names, characters, places, and events are products of the author's imagination, and any resemblance to actual events or places or persons, living or dead, is entirely coincidental.

🪔ALADDIN
An imprint of Simon & Schuster Children's Publishing Division
1230 Avenue of the Americas, New York, New York 10020
First Aladdin paperback edition August 2021
Text copyright © 2021 by Joseph McGee
Illustrations copyright © 2021 by Teo Skaffa
Also available in an Aladdin hardcover edition.
All rights reserved, including the right of reproduction in whole or in part in any form.
ALADDIN and related logo are registered trademarks of Simon & Schuster, Inc.
For information about special discounts for bulk purchases, please contact Simon & Schuster Special Sales at 1-866-506-1949 or business@simonandschuster.com.
The Simon & Schuster Speakers Bureau can bring authors to your live event. For more information or to book an event contact the Simon & Schuster Speakers Bureau at 1-866-248-3049 or visit our website at www.simonspeakers.com.
Designed by Tiara Iandiorio
The text of this book was set in Adobe Garamond Pro.
Manufactured in the United States of America 1021 OFF
10 9 8 7 6 5 4 3 2
Library of Congress Control Number 2020952998
ISBN 9781534480896 (hc)
ISBN 9781534480889 (pbk)
ISBN 9781534480902 (ebook)

For Donna Galanti and Keith Strunk.

And also for Ron Burgundy; the original

Magnum, P.I.; Ron Swanson; and my dad—

gentlemen, your mustaches

are an inspiration.

Greetings, friends . . . You have opened this book because you are interested in the unknown, the strange, the unexplainable. Well, look no further. For the first time ever, I am prepared to share the shocking and spooky tale of what happened in the curious and quirky town of Wolver Hollow. I must warn you, though. . . . What you are about to read is not for the faint of heart. Continue if you dare . . . but do not say you weren't warned.

". . . And his mustache was all that
remained."

Mr. Noffler leaned against the edge of his
desk and watched the class. They were silent
for a moment. Their eyes were wide. None of
the students knew whether or not to believe
what they'd just heard.

Every kid in Wolver Hollow grew up going
through the same weird routine on October

19, but until now, they never knew why. Every October 19, the town shut down before dusk.

Shops closed.

Parents made their children stay inside.

Curtains were drawn.

And doors were bolted.

Every year, men who were normally clean-shaven grew mustaches in preparation for October 19. Women and children took their fake mustaches out of the drawer and taped them above their lips. Parents made a game of it, but their eyes were filled with fear.

When children would ask why they had to wear mustaches, or what Mommy was so afraid of, it was always the same answer: "You're too young" or "It's nothing, just a silly old legend." But now that they were in fifth grade, they were finally learning the truth. They were finally going to hear about the legend of October 19.

"And that is today's local history lesson," said Mr. Noffler. He clapped his hands and sat down.

Parker frowned. That couldn't be it, he thought. He had the feeling that Mr. Noffler was leaving out all of the good parts. He hadn't told them why it was all such a big deal in the first place. He hadn't told them why they locked their doors and wore fake mustaches. Parker sensed a mystery, and he wanted answers. He was not about to let Mr. Noffler stop there. Not when he was so close to learning the truth. Parker leaned forward at his desk and raised his hand as high as he could.

"Yes, Parker?" said Mr. Noffler. He set down his marker and adjusted his glasses.

"How *big* was the explosion?" asked Parker.

"So big," said Mr. Noffler, "that it rattled houses and broke windows for miles around. It left a crater in the ground large enough that our entire school could fit inside of it!"

The class murmured in amazement.

"Well, how did the gunpowder explode?" Parker asked.

Mr. Noffler tapped his upper lip, like he always did when he was considering his answer. Mr. Noffler did not normally have a mustache, but, like everyone else, this week he did. October 19 was only one day away. He crossed his arms and stared at Parker.

"That's a great question, Parker," said Mr.

Noffler. "No one ever quite figured out what caused the unfortunate black powder incident that vaporized poor old Bockius Beauregard. It was labeled an accident."

"Vaporized?" Parker asked.

"Vaporized," said Mr. Noffler. "Well . . . mostly. As I said—"

"The mustache," said Lucas, Parker's best friend. "It survived."

"Yes, the mustache," said Mr. Noffler. "The magnificent mustache of Bockius Beauregard. It was the envy of every man in town."

"That must have been some mustache," said Gilbert Blardle, doodling mustaches in the margin of his notebook.

"Indeed it was," said Mr. Noffler. "There never was another mustache quite so magnificent ever recorded again in Wolver Hollow."

"Who keeps track of mustaches?" asked Lucas.

"This is the weirdest town ever," said Parker.

"Some say that mustache had a life of its own," continued Mr. Noffler. "Some say that that is why it returns from the grave every year on the anniversary of Bockius Beauregard's unfortunate explosion. Nobody knows for certain. Nobody dares to go looking. And so, it remains . . . a mystery."

A mystery! Parker's eyes lit up. He knew it!

"Wait," said Parker. "Did you just say that the mustache returns? From the grave?"

Mr. Noffler smiled and stood up from his desk. "I did."

"Are you getting all of this?" Lucas asked.

"Every word," said Parker, writing furiously on a piece of paper. He and Lucas had a detective agency—the Midnight Owl Detective Agency—and finding out if the haunted mustache was real or not sounded like a mystery most definitely worth pursuing.

"This could be our biggest case yet," said Lucas.

"Bigger than the Case of the Missing Toad," said Parker.

"Or the Mysterious Mailbox Mix-Up!" Lucas said.

Mr. Noffler slipped his thumbs through his suspenders and slowly walked about the classroom. He weaved his way around the groups of tables.

"His mustache," said Mr. Noffler, "was

indeed all that remained. It was found six hundred yards—five football fields—away from the crater, in an apple orchard. It was still attached to his lip."

"Gross!" said Sally McKinley, who sat across from Parker.

Parker wrote, *Five football fields. Still attached to lip.*

"It's not true, you know," said Samantha von Oppelstein. She was applying a new coat of black nail polish to her fingernails.

"What isn't?" Parker asked. He tried to listen to Mr. Noffler and write down everything Mr. Noffler said at the same time. He already had one full page of notes from what Mr. Noffler had told them at the beginning of class.

"All of it," she said, not looking up.

"How do you know?" Parker asked.

She shrugged. "It's just a stupid story."

Parker stared at his notes. This was the coolest thing he'd ever heard. He didn't want it to be just some stupid story. He wanted this to be the Midnight Owl Detective Agency's biggest case yet.

"Well, I think you're wrong," he said. "I think the legend is true. I think the mustache does return from the grave every year."

"Oh yeah?" she asked. "Then why, in over

one hundred years, has the mustache never been seen?"

Parker opened his mouth to answer, then snapped it shut. He tapped his chin with his pencil. He tried to answer again, but closed his mouth. He looked like a fish, sucking in air.

"You heard what Mr. Noffler said," Parker finally managed to say. "Nobody dares to go look for it." But even he was not convinced by that answer.

Samantha von Oppelstein rolled her eyes. "Uh-huh, right. Suit yourself. But how could a mustache survive an explosion that big when the rest of the man was . . . What was the word?"

"Vaporized," said Parker, checking his notes.

"Vaporized," finished Samantha von Oppelstein. "It's impossible."

Parker read back through his notes. She had a point. It did seem rather improbable. Not impossible, he thought, but highly improbable.

Robby Dugan raised his hand and said what they were all thinking. "That's impossible. A mustache can't go flying six football fields away."

"Can't it?" Mr. Noffler asked.

Nobody had an answer.

"It's all true," said Mr. Noffler. "You can read about it in the town archives, in the library. Some poor farmer out picking apples scooped up what he thought was a caterpillar—"

"Mr. Noffler, stop!" squealed Lucinda Brown from the other side of the room. "I'm going to be sick."

But Mr. Noffler did not stop.

"—only to realize he was holding the magnificent mustache of Bockius Beauregard. Killed the old man on the spot. He had a heart attack right there. But the farmer was only the first victim."

The class fell silent.

"See?" Parker said to Samantha von Oppelstein. "There was another victim. That means that it came back. From the *grave*."

Samantha von Oppelstein painted another nail and said nothing.

Parker frowned. Why was she being so difficult?

"When they found the farmer's body, still holding that bloody mustache, they asked the same thing you asked. 'How could

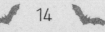

a mustache survive such an explosion?' They called it unnatural. They said it was the devil's work, and they blamed the mustache for the farmer's death."

"So what did they do?" Lucas asked.

"They pried that bloody mustache out of the farmer's cold, dead hand and took it up to the cemetery. There they found a spot in the farthest, most weed-choked section of the graveyard, and they dug a small hole. Then they set that mustache on fire, and when it was nothing but a pile of ashes, they dumped those ashes in the hole, covered them over, and left them to the worms and grubs."

"Cool," said Samantha von Oppelstein. "This is why I like to write poetry in the graveyard. It's quite eerie."

"You," Parker said to Samantha von Oppel-stein, "are odd."

"Thank you."

"And one year later," said Mr. Noffler, "on October 19, the very anniversary of the explosion, they found the cemetery caretaker lying dead among the tombstones. . . . Something had tried to steal his upper lip."

The class gasped.

"Steal it?" asked Parker.

"Steal it," said Mr. Noffler.

"His whole lip?" Lucas asked.

"The whole thing," said Mr. Noffler.

The class gasped again.

"But that caretaker had a bit of a mustache of his own," explained Mr. Noffler. "A pencil-thin one, popular back then, and so the magnificent

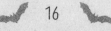

mustache of Bockius Beauregard could not steal the caretaker's lip. That is why today, on the anniversary of Bockius's death, the people of Wolver Hollow wear mustaches. It's why we stay inside, and stay safe. Because, you see . . . that magnificent mustache haunts Wolver Hollow, angry at being blown up, burned, blamed for the farmer's death, and dumped in a hole. That magnificent, remarkable mustache, unable to rest in peace, forever seeks a new lip to rest upon. And if it finds you late at night, when the moon is out and the crickets stop chirping—"

The entire fifth-grade class sat at the edge of their seats.

They gripped the edge of their desks.

They watched Mr. Noffler with wide-open, unblinking eyes.

"—it will STEAL YOUR LIP FOR ITS OWN!" yelled Mr. Noffler, leaping toward them.

Several students screamed, most jumped, and three students fell out of their chairs. But not Parker. Parker was thinking. Samantha von Oppelstein had asked a very good question. Why had it not been seen in all of these years? Was there really a haunted mustache, or was it just some silly old superstition? He and Lucas would get to the bottom of this and discover the truth. But there was only one way to do that.

The bell rang, and with a scraping of chairs and shuffling of feet, Mr. Noffler's fifth-grade class hurried out the door.

"Remember to stay indoors tomorrow night!" Mr. Noffler called out to them. "Be sure to wear your mustaches!"

Parker stopped Lucas in the hallway. "Meet me by the bike rack," he said. "We have a mystery on our hands."

Lucas grinned. "The Midnight Owl Detective Agency is on the case," he said.

Parker had his backpack on and his bike

ready to go when Lucas got to the bike rack.

"What was Samantha von Oppelstein going on about?" Lucas asked. He climbed onto his bike. "I saw her whispering something to you."

"She says the whole legend isn't true," said Parker. "She says it's impossible."

"It does seem kind of impossible," Lucas said.

"Improbable, not impossible," Parker said. "There's a difference."

"But if it *were* true, you'd think that the mustache would have found at least one lip in the last one-hundred-something years," Lucas said. "You'd think someone would have seen it at least once."

"That's what she said. But if it weren't true, why would the town shut down on October 19? Why would everyone lock their doors and bolt their windows? Why would everyone be so scared?"

"Superstition?" said Lucas.

Parker flipped his kickstand up and started pedaling.

"Come on," he said.

"Where are we going?" asked Lucas, pedaling behind him.

"The library," said Parker. "Mr. Noffler said we could find the records there. Any good case begins with studying the facts."

Lucas groaned. The library was the last place he wanted to be on a Friday afternoon. Okay, second-to-last place. The cemetery was the first, and that's exactly where they'd have to go tomorrow night if they were going to find out whether or not the mustache was real.

Parker and Lucas pedaled down South Main Street. They crossed over the old metal bridge that spanned Wolf Creek. They leaned as far to the left as they could and spit over the short wall and into the fast-moving creek. Everyone knew that a troll lived under the bridge, and if you didn't spit when you crossed, he'd curse you and eat your toes in the night.

They passed by people on the sidewalk—men with mustaches, ladies already wearing their fake mustaches even though the anniversary wasn't until tomorrow. People hurried about their business. Nobody stopped to chat with their neighbors like they normally did. Everyone was in a rush. They offered brisk nods or a quick hello, and were on their way.

Silverman's Pharmacy had a big sign in the window offering AUTHENTIC HORSEHAIR MUSTACHES for two dollars, while Kate's Craft Emporium had Make Your Own Mustache kits marked down, WHILE SUPPLIES LAST.

The boys said hello to Mayor Stine as they passed. He was in the middle of supervising the hanging of a large banner that stretched over the street, from the library on one side to town hall on the other.

It read: CURFEW IN EFFECT, TOMORROW, OCTOBER 19. DUSK TO DAWN!

He pointed to his thick, drooping mustache and called after the boys, "Don't forget your mustaches."

"We won't!" they called back, coasting up to the front of the library.

The library was a big, tall brick building with two marble pillars on either side of the arched front double doors. Ivy raced up one side of the building, and the grass was in definite need of being mowed. Parker and Lucas rested their bikes against the rusted metal fence and climbed the steep steps. Two dark semicircular front windows made the building look like it had eyes, angry eyes just waiting for kids to approach the front doors and be swallowed whole.

Parker pulled the doors open, and he and Lucas stepped into the dimly lit library. Dark wood shelves created a maze of books that seemed to stretch forever. A few empty chairs and tables were scattered about, and a broad set of stairs curved up to a railing-enclosed balcony with even more books. Dim lamps cast shadows across the rugs and runners, and creepy old men and women stared down at them from their framed paintings on the walls.

"Aren't libraries supposed to be relaxing?" Lucas asked. "It feels like this is where books go to die."

"Smells funny too," said Parker. "Like my grandfather's socks."

"Why do you know what your grandfather's socks smell like?"

"Because he won't wear shoes."

"Can I help you, boys?" asked a short, ancient-looking woman peering down at them from the balcony. She lifted her glasses and squinted at Parker and Lucas, then dropped the glasses back into place.

"Yes, ma'am," said Parker. "We're doing a research project for school—"

Lucas nudged him. "Don't lie," he whispered.

Parker turned and whispered back, "It's not a lie. We're doing research, and it's because of school."

"What kind of research?" asked the old

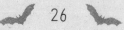 26

woman, suddenly standing behind them.

"Ahh! How did you . . . ? You were just—" Parker pointed at the balcony and then at the floor. "Never mind. We're interested in reading more about the big quarry explosion of eighteen hundred something."

"Yeah," said Lucas, "the one that exploded a mustache."

The ancient librarian chuckled. "Oh no," she said, "it didn't explode a mustache."

"It didn't?" Parker asked. "But—"

"Oh, heavens no," she said. "It exploded a *man*. His mustache—"

"Was all that remained," Parker said. "Of course."

"That's right," she said, smiling. "Terrible business, and dangerous, too. Come with me."

The librarian led them to a small room at the back of the library. A red velvet rope hung across the open doorway, and a hanging sign read: ARCHIVES. LIBRARY STAFF ONLY.

She lifted the rope and ushered them in.

"Have a seat. What you want is the *Wolver Hollow Gazette*, years 1887 to 1889. Just a moment."

Parker and Lucas waited while she rolled a ladder over to a particularly dusty, particularly cobwebbed section of shelves. The librarian climbed up to the very top and reached for the highest shelf.

"Nobody ever reads the history anymore," she said. "You might be surprised how many secrets this old town holds. Ah, here we are."

She slipped a large book off the shelf and slowly climbed back down. She set it on the table in front of the boys with a loud thud. An inch of dust rose up off the table.

Lucas and Parker both tried not to sneeze.

"October 19, 1888," she said, shuffling out of the room. "And don't touch anything else. I'll know."

She stopped and peered back around the corner.

"I always know."

Parker and Lucas stared at the open

doorway. Neither of them was sure what to say.

"Always know!" said the librarian, popping her head around the corner again and then slipping back into the hallway. "Always know . . . ," she said. Her voice trailed down the hallway, away from them.

Parker and Lucas waited to make sure she wasn't going to poke her head back in, before they said anything.

"How'd she get down from the balcony so quick?" Parker whispered.

"Who cares," said Lucas. "Let's just check the story and get out of here. This place gives me the creeps."

Parker opened the creaky old book. Pages and pages of age-yellowed newspaper clippings had been carefully placed in protective plastic. A centipede slithered out from the binding, and Lucas nearly screamed.

"*Scutigera coleoptrata*," said Parker. "Common house centipede."

"You know I hate bugs, Parker," said Lucas.

"It's gone," said Parker, turning the pages. "Here it is, October 19, 1888. Look! It's the front-page article."

The headline read *Quarry Explosion Rocks Wolver Hollow*, and underneath that was a grainy photograph of a man standing before what must have been the black powder storehouse. He stared directly at the boys.

"It's so hard to see anything," said Lucas. "The photo is so old!"

"Hold on, I've got just the thing," said

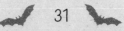

31

Parker. He reached into his pocket and took out a small magnifying glass. It had been a gift from his aunt Clementine Foggbottom to help him with his detective work. And for looking at bugs. Parker fancied himself a bit of an entomologist.

Parker leaned forward and studied the picture. It wasn't the man's dark eyes, or the tall hat he held in his hand, or even the caption that read *Bockius Beauregard, longtime quarry employee, was, unfortunately, exploded.* No, what caught Parker's attention was his mustache. It was, indeed, a magnificent mustache. Mr. Noffler had not been exaggerating.

It was thick and full, completely hiding his upper lip. But not one whisker dared grow longer than any other. Every. Single. Hair. Was

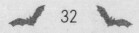

trimmed, in line, with the hairs to the right and the left of it. Bockius's mustache stretched from ear to ear in a breathtaking swoop of precisely waxed curls. Starting from right under each nostril, Bockius's mustache was like a gentle ski slope, a downhill ride that suddenly became a complete corkscrew, a roller coaster that turned upside down and back out again, in a loop so defined, so exact, that you could place a nickel in that space and it would fit there perfectly.

Bockius Beauregard's mustache was truly something to behold.

"Let me have a look," said Lucas.

Parker handed the magnifying glass over, and Lucas scooted closer to the book.

"He doesn't look very happy in this picture."

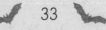

"I don't think anyone was happy back then," said Parker. "Who could be happy when you had to go out back to a wooden outhouse in the middle of winter to poop?"

"Good point," said Lucas. He read through the rest of the article. "Well, Mr. Noffler's story checks out. The explosion was as big as he said, and the mustache was really all that remained."

"Let me see," said Parker. He slid the book closer and turned a few pages. "Here's an article about his memorial service." Parker and Lucas leaned in, reading the old print.

Parker stopped and tapped at one line in particular. *Nothing could ever get between him and his mustache*, read the article. *"I'd sooner be caught dead than to be without my mustache,"*

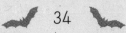

said Bockius Beauregard, days before the unfor-tunate accident in which he was exploded.

Lucas read the next line aloud. "'Mr. Beauregard, of Hill Crest Manor, was known to apply one tin of Handsome Hank's mustache wax to his magnificent mustache weekly.'"

"Well, that's just it!" said Parker.

"What is?"

"We need some Handsome Hank's," Parker said. "*If* there is a haunted mustache, it stands to reason that it comes back as a ghost because it can't rest, right? I'll bet it appears by the grave of Bockius Beauregard, right?"

"Okay, that makes sense," said Lucas. "And when . . . *if* we find it there, then what?"

"We'd need something to put it at ease," Parker said. "Something to connect it to its former life so it doesn't have to be restless anymore. I'll bet Handsome Hank's mustache wax would put the ghost to rest and stop it from haunting Wolver Hollow."

"Where are we supposed to get Handsome Hank's mustache wax?" Lucas asked.

Parker shrugged. "The pharmacy?"

"You think it's that simple?"

"Maybe the ghost won't be angry anymore. Maybe it'll be reminded of Bockius and it can finally rest in peace. A happy, no-longer-haunted mustache."

Lucas was about to say something else, something about the old Hill Crest Manor, but the grainy picture of the memorial service caught his attention. He took the magnifying glass from Parker and got so close to the old article that his nose touched the book.

"Isn't that the librarian?" he asked, sitting back up. "In the picture?"

Parker was just about to have a look for himself when the librarian's voice startled them.

"You boys find everything you were looking for?" she asked. She took the book from them and closed it.

"You have to stop doing that!" Parker said.

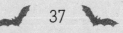 37

"Doing what, dear?"

"Sneaking up on us," said Lucas.

She just smiled and leaned in closer. She smelled a bit like rotten eggs, like that sulfur smell from chemistry class. Lucas thought he saw that centipede slide around the back of her ear and crawl up into her hair.

Parker tapped the table.

"It's just an old legend, right?" he asked the librarian as she climbed the ladder to the top shelf.

"Is it?" she said.

"If it's not a legend, then why has no one died since then?" Parker asked.

She slid the book back into place. "How do you know they haven't?"

Parker and Lucas gulped.

"Why has no one seen it?" Lucas asked.

"Who says they haven't?" said the librarian.

The boys got goose bumps.

"How do we stop it from trying to steal our lips if we're just trying to help it?" Parker asked.

"You boys ask a lot of questions," she said. "I'd suggest you read *Lester's Lore and Legends*, but it's already been checked out. I'll tell you this, though. Most spirits just want their old life back, or at least some part of it."

Parker nudged Lucas. "See? Handsome Hank's mustache wax."

"If the mustache can't have Bockius," the librarian continued, "perhaps it would settle for its old home."

"Hill Crest Manor," Parker and Lucas said at the same time.

The old librarian grinned. "But first you'd have to get it there."

"How do you know all of this?" asked Lucas.

The old librarian grinned wider. "I read."

She escorted the boys out of the archives and closed the velvet rope behind them.

They thanked her for helping them and made their way to the front doors.

"Old Giroux's cabin," she said, just as Parker was about to open the front door.

The boys turned, unsure what she was talking about.

"That's where the records are," she said. "That's how you'll find Bockius's grave. A boy can get into all sorts of trouble wandering around a cemetery at night. Best he knows where he's going when he's got business to attend to. Good luck."

Parker nodded. Lucas tugged at his elbow, and they stepped out of the dark library and into the light of the late-afternoon sun.

"I am never going in there again," said Lucas.

Parker glanced behind them. The librarian stood in the window watching them.

"Me neither," said Parker.

3

They walked their bikes down the
street in silence for a bit. They passed the pet
store, with a litter of black kittens in the window. The kittens hissed and spit and clawed
the air as the boys walked past. Church Street
was just a block ahead, and the entrance to the
old cemetery was at the end of it.

"Do you believe any of what she said?"
Lucas asked. "And did you get a look at that

last picture? I swear that was the librarian. But she didn't look a day different!"

"I don't know about any of it," said Parker. "But I suppose that's why it's a mystery. *If* the mustache is real, it seems most likely that it will appear at Bockius's grave tomorrow night. *If* it appears, we can lure it with some Handsome Hank's mustache wax back to Hill Crest Manor."

"Then what?" Lucas asked. "How do we put it to rest? Do we just hand over the mustache wax and say 'See ya later, ghost mustache. Have a good night. Please stop haunting our town'?"

"I'll bet that book would tell us," Parker said. "*Lester's Lore and Legends*."

"But you heard the librarian. It's checked out."

"I think I know who checked it out."

"Who?" Lucas asked.

Parker clapped Lucas on the shoulder. "Think about it. Who else would bother to check out a book on spirits and monsters?"

"You?"

"Samantha von Oppelstein!" said Parker. "She must have checked it out. She was just telling me how she likes to write poetry in the cemetery."

"That's odd," said Lucas.

"That's what I said!" Parker said.

A police car drove by slowly, and Sheriff Macklin stared at them through his mirrored sunglasses. Lucas and Parker waited until he passed before continuing. The way he looked at them, it was as if he somehow knew what

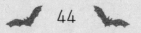

they were conspiring about. Or maybe they were just being paranoid.

"What about the curfew?" asked Lucas.

"We'll have to be careful," said Parker. "You can sleep over my house tomorrow night, and we'll sneak out from there."

"Parker, how am I supposed to convince my parents to let me sleep over tomorrow night? They'll never let me out of the house on October 19!"

"I'm sure you'll think of something. Meet me at the gazebo tomorrow at noon." Parker hopped on his bike and pedaled down Second Street. "And bring whatever money you have," he called over his shoulder. "We need to buy some Handsome Hank's!"

❂ ❂ ❂

The gazebo was not empty when Lucas arrived the next day. Samantha von Oppelstein sat on the railing, reading through an old black book.

"Hey," said Lucas. He looked around for Parker. "You haven't seen—"

"Parker?" she asked, not looking up.

"Yeah."

"No."

"I'm supposed to meet him here," said Lucas. "Detective business."

"I know."

"You know?" Lucas laid his bike in the grass. "How do you know?"

"He told me," she said. "Asked me to meet him here too."

Lucas tried to see what she was reading. "Is that—"

"*Lester's Lore and Legends*? Yes."

Parker turned the corner of Pine and Mill, pedaling toward them. Lucas breathed a sigh of relief. He had no idea what to say to Samantha von Oppelstein, and she seemed more interested in the book than in talking with him.

"You came," said Parker. He coasted up to the gazebo.

"I said I would, didn't I?" said Samantha von Oppelstein. "So, let's hear it." She closed the book, slid off the railing, and leaned on the inside of the gazebo. "What's the Midnight Owl Detective Agency up to?"

"Well, it's like this," Parker began, and he told her everything they'd learned in the library yesterday and what they planned to

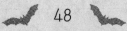

do. "But once we get the mustache to Hill Crest Manor, we don't know what to do."

"And the librarian said the answers were in that book," Lucas said.

"Then you're in luck," said Samantha von Oppelstein.

"We are?" Parker and Lucas asked at the same time.

"Yep," she said. She hugged the book against her. "But I want in."

"In what?" asked Parker.

"The Midnight Owl Detective Agency?" Lucas asked.

"Yep," she said. "In on the agency and in on this case."

"But you said you didn't believe the legend," Parker said.

"The agency isn't for girls . . . ," Lucas sputtered. "I mean, the agency is just—"

"Well, then I guess you won't know how to get rid of your ghost," she said. She took two steps toward the gazebo exit.

"Wait, wait, wait," said Parker.

Samantha von Oppelstein stopped and looked at the boys. She raised one eyebrow.

"Yes?"

"You can help us with the case," Parker said.

"And?" she asked. One corner of her mouth rose in a slight smirk.

Parker nudged Lucas in the ribs.

"You can join the detective agency," Lucas said.

Samantha von Oppelstein smiled. "Good. Then here's what we need to do. . . ."

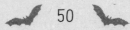

According to what Samantha von Oppelstein had read in *Lester's Lore and Legends*, once the restless ghost was drawn to the last place it called home, it had to be trapped in a circle of salt, in full view of the rising sun. Once the sunlight fell upon the spirit, it would find peace and never again be able to rise from the dead and haunt the living.

"So all we need now is some salt and a tin of Handsome Hank's mustache wax!" Parker said.

Samantha von Oppelstein volunteered to bring the salt, and Parker and Lucas scraped together the change and few crumpled dollar

bills they had to buy the mustache wax at Silverman's Pharmacy.

"You're in luck," said Mr. Silverman, handing them a tin of Handsome Hank's mustache wax: GUARANTEED TO SHAPE YOUR 'STACHE! "Last tin left. Now you kids better get home and get inside."

Mr. Silverman closed the door behind them and flipped the sign from OPEN to CLOSED.

"Hill Crest Manor is haunted, you know," Samantha von Oppelstein said as they walked their bikes along the sidewalk.

"So is the cemetery," said Lucas.

"I suppose we shall see soon enough," said Parker, turning down his street. "Samantha, Lucas and I will meet you at the sign on the edge of town when the sun goes down."

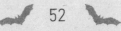

"Don't chicken out," she said.

"As if!" said Lucas.

"Oh, we'll be there, mustaches, mustache wax, and all," said Parker. "Don't forget the salt."

Samantha von Oppelstein gave them two thumbs up and turned down the sidewalk in the opposite direction.

"Parker?" said Lucas.

"Yes?"

"I've got a very bad feeling about this."

A slight gust of wind kicked up, swirling a pile of autumn leaves, and overhead, dark clouds began to form.

Lucas managed to convince his parents
to let him stay at Parker's house as long as
he promised to wear his mustache and to
stay inside.

"Well, you'll only be breaking *one* of those
promises," Parker said. "You *will* be wearing
your mustache."

"I don't like breaking *any* of those promises," Lucas said, trying his mustache on in the

mirror. He reached for the tin of Handsome
Hank's, but Parker pulled it away.

"You can't use this!" he said. "We need a full
and complete tin in order to lure that mustache
to Hill Crest Manor. And you're going to have
to break the second promise. We already told

Samantha von Oppelstein we'd be there, and if we don't show up, she'll think we're chickens. Even worse, she'll be out there, alone, when the mustache is on the hunt."

"*If* there's a mustache," said Lucas.

"*If* the mustache exists," Parker agreed. "If it doesn't, then the Midnight Owl Detective Agency can put this case to rest and prove to the town that October 19 is no longer a date to be terrified of."

After dinner, the boys waited in Parker's room until it was dark. The plan had been to wait until Parker's mom sat down in the living room to watch television, before slipping out Parker's bedroom window and down the ivy-covered trellis. That way she wouldn't see them from the kitchen window. But tonight, of all nights, she decided to put together a puzzle at the kitchen table.

"What do we do now?" Lucas asked.

"We just have to wait," Parker said, peeking around the corner of the kitchen doorway. "Every once in a while she decides to do a puzzle. This appears to be a thousand-piece puzzle. She'll be frustrated in half an hour, forty-five minutes tops, and then give up and go watch TV. Happens all the time."

Parker and Lucas watched the clouds get darker and angrier, unable to do anything but think about what may be waiting for them in the cemetery. Finally, as Parker had predicted, his mom gave a very loud and frustrated sigh. Her footsteps clicked across the wood floor, and the television snapped on.

"Go time," said Parker.

He slipped his bedroom window open, and the boys quietly climbed out. They crawled along the porch roof and then down the ivy-covered trellis. Once on the ground, they dared a peek through the living room window. Parker's mom sat on the couch, watching some old black-and-white television show. The light from the TV cast her shadow, and the shadow of her fake mustache, on the wall behind her.

"Let's go," Parker whispered. He shouldered his backpack. It was filled with gloves, bug spray, flashlights, extra batteries, and a tin of Handsome Hank's mustache wax: GUARANTEED TO SHAPE YOUR 'STACHE!

"Hold on," said Lucas. He pressed his mustache harder against his face. "How's it look?"

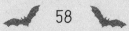

"Good," Parker whispered. "Mine?"

"Perfect," said Lucas.

"Oh, almost forgot . . ." Parker reached back into his bag and took out two cardboard Midnight Owl Detective Agency badges that he'd made. He pinned one to his shirt with the attached safety pin. "Figured that a case this big deserved a badge."

"Cool!" said Lucas.

"Now we're official," Parker said.

They hopped on their bikes and pedaled away from Parker's house. Despite the clouds, the moon was bright, just the kind of moon Mr. Noffler had warned them about.

"Hear that?" Lucas asked.

"Hear what?" asked Parker. He listened a second. "Crickets."

"Crickets," said Lucas.

Parker remembered what Mr. Noffler had said.

When the moon is out and the crickets stop chirping . . .

"Never thought I'd be so happy to hear crickets," Lucas said.

"Agreed," said Parker. "And we won't be needing our flashlights, at least."

"Until we get inside that haunted manor," said Lucas, shivering.

The moonlit night cast shadows over the tall pines that seemed to stretch across the empty streets like inky skeleton fingers. Somewhere a cat screeched, some dogs barked, and a raccoon rattling around in a trash can almost made Lucas crash into Parker.

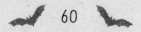

60

The boys pedaled down the road out of town, where the woods got thicker and darker, and the houses and buildings all but disappeared. This was the edge of the wild, the road north into the hills and mountains. Parker's plan was to sneak over the cemetery wall closest to the old windmill, away from anyone who might see them if they tried to climb the wall closer to town.

The sign was just up ahead, right past the old dirt road that cut up toward the Pine Knob Lodge Resort. It marked the edge of town, and anyone driving out this way would read, NOW LEAVING WOLVER HOLLOW, VERMONT, A QUAINT PLACE TO HANG YOUR HAT.

Parker and Lucas pulled off the road and peered into the shadows. This was where they'd agreed to meet Samantha von Oppel-stein, but Samantha von Oppelstein was nowhere to be seen.

"Samantha?" Parker whispered. "Samantha von Oppelstein?"

Nothing. Only a low rumble of thunder. Even the bright moon could not penetrate the gloom of the forest. It smelled of dead leaves and damp soil. Any manner of creature might be lurking behind the trees, waiting at the edge of the darkness. Anything could rush out and suddenly be upon them: a bear, a wolf, a windigo . . .

"I knew she'd chicken out," Lucas said. He dropped his bike near the sign.

"Boo!" shouted a voice from the darkness.

Lucas shrieked. Parker fell from his bike

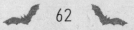

and landed on his butt in a pile of muddy leaves.

"You should have seen the looks on your faces!" said Samantha von Oppelstein, stepping out of the woods. "That was priceless."

"Real funny," said Parker, wiping the mud off his hands.

"Bring the salt, at least?" Lucas asked. He helped Parker to his feet.

Samantha von Oppelstein pulled a full container of

salt out of her bag and shook it in the air.

"Nice badge," she said. She pointed to the Midnight Owl Detective Agency badge on Parker's shirt.

Parker smiled. He was very proud of the badges he'd made.

The boys left their bikes by the sign, and the three of them crept toward the tall stone wall that surrounded the cemetery. The moon hung in the sky like a pale, bloated spider over the rickety old windmill. Every once in a while, the giant wood fans would move just a little, creaking and groaning. Old Giroux, the cemetery caretaker, lived in a little cabin next to the windmill. The location of Bockius's grave would be in the records, in that cabin. If they found those, and if the legend were true, they'd also find the haunted mustache.

"This wall is way taller up close," said Lucas. "It doesn't look so big from a distance."

"I wonder," said Samantha von Oppelstein, "if the wall is here to keep people out . . . or to keep things *in*?"

"Not cool," Lucas said. "Not cool at all."

Somewhere in the woods a wolf howled. The air held that brisk, fresh scent of rain even though the storm looked a ways off.

Parker was the better climber (he'd climbed the cargo net in gym class the third fastest), so he went first. He got up on top of the wall with a little boost from Lucas.

Samantha von Oppelstein went next, and then finally Lucas. Samantha von Oppelstein and Parker stretched their hands down and

pulled him up. Parker tossed his bag down, and then all three of them dropped down into the graveyard.

The old gravestones poked out of the ground like chipped teeth. Here and there a faded statue of an angel or a large cross stood out. A cloud passed before the moon, and the cemetery was bathed in darkness for just a moment.

Parker put his finger over his lips and pointed toward Old Giroux's crooked little cabin sitting next to the sagging windmill. "I have to get in there to find where Bockius is buried. Otherwise we'll be out here all night."

Samantha von Oppelstein nudged Lucas. "Lucas and I will draw him out," she whispered.

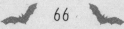

"We will?" Lucas asked.

"Yeah," she said. "We'll create a distraction."

"What kind of distraction are—"

Before Parker could finish, Samantha von Oppelstein stood up, cupped her hands around her mouth, and hollered, "Booooooooooo! I am a haunted mustache!"

"Are you out of your mind?" Lucas asked. The front door of the cabin swung open, and a lanky figure stood at the threshold.

"Who's out there?" called a gravelly, old voice.

"Just us mustaches!" Samantha von Oppelstein called out. She turned to Parker. "There's your distraction."

"Show yourselves!" Old Giroux hollered. He held a lantern up high and scanned the cemetery. "You're in big trouble, whoever you are! Big trouble indeed!"

"Run!" Samantha von Oppelstein shouted, pulling Lucas along with her.

Lucas and Samantha von Oppelstein ran from the cabin, deeper into the graveyard, as Old Giroux charged out of his house.

Parker ducked down behind the tall gravestone of Wilfred Cooke, A KINDER FELLOW YOU'LL NEVER MEET, UNLESS YOU DIG DOWN ABOUT SIX FEET, and waited for Old Giroux to pass.

"Darned kids!" Old Giroux snarled. "You think you can outrun Giroux? I'll show you what happens to trespassers in *my* graveyard! And on *this* night of all nights?"

Parker waited until Old Giroux was well

past him before standing up and running toward the cabin.

"You're going to wish that mustache got you, once I get my hands on you!" Old Giroux hollered at Lucas and Samantha von Oppelstein, stomping after them in his mud-caked boots.

Parker reached the open door of Old Giroux's cabin, took a deep breath, and then slipped inside.

5

Old Giroux's cabin was small and
cramped. The heads of all the different animals
he'd hunted adorned the walls, staring down
at Parker: deer, wolf, elk, bear, badger. There
was even a large boar with tusks so long, you
could hang a hat on them, just like the town
sign said. *A quaint place to hang your hat.* But
Giroux's cabin wasn't quaint; it was creepy.

Open cans of beans and stacks of mail-order catalogs sat on the small kitchen table. An old television with an antenna squatted atop milk crates, and a hammock strung up in one corner appeared to be his bed.

It smelled like sweaty socks and spoiled milk. Parker held his nose. The wolf head's eyes seemed to glow, and Parker swore that it was watching him.

"Look, I'm just getting some information, and I'll be gone," he whispered to the wolf's head.

A bookshelf against the wall was filled with moss-green ledgers. Parker was willing to bet that those ledgers were exactly what he was after.

The floorboards groaned and creaked under Parker's steps, and even though Old Giroux was not there to hear him, Parker could not help but cringe with every noisy step. The ledgers were

lined up in long rows, arranged by years. Parker slid his finger across them until he found the ledger for years 1850 to 1900.

"Bingo," Parker said. He slipped the book off the shelf and wiped away the cobwebs.

Somewhere out there Old Giroux was chasing Lucas and Samantha von Oppelstein through the graveyard, and it was only a matter of time before the caretaker gave up and came back. Parker had to hurry.

He flipped through the pages until he found the year 1888. He traced down the list,

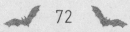

month by month, until he reached October. There he was: Bockius Beauregard.

Parker slipped a pen out of his pocket, pulled the cap off with his teeth, and scribbled the burial plot on his hand: *C113.*

"See?" Parker said to the wolf's head. "That was it. I won't bother you anymore."

A lantern bobbed along in the darkness, and Old Giroux's muttering grew dangerously close.

". . . think they can make a fool out of Old Giroux, do they?"

Parker had just slipped through the front door and around the side of the cabin when the old man appeared.

"Serves 'em right if the mustache gets 'em," said Old Giroux. Parker hurried away

from the cabin, back toward where he and the others had split up.

"Psst, Parker," said Lucas. "Over here."

Lucas and Samantha von Oppelstein were crouched down behind a statue of an angel.

"Get it?" Lucas asked.

"C113," said Parker. "Good job, you two."

"I know exactly where that section is," said Samantha von Oppelstein. "It's in the back corner of the graveyard. Come on."

Samantha von Oppelstein led Parker and Lucas through the cemetery. Despite the bright moon, both boys stumbled several times on broken and half-buried gravestones. But not Samantha von Oppelstein.

"I know this place like the back of my hand," she said.

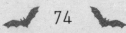

Thunder rumbled overhead, and a jagged arc of lightning flashed across the sky.

"Where's your mustache?" Lucas asked Samantha von Oppelstein.

"Oh yeah!"

She fished around in her bag until she found it.

"Mustache on a stick," she said. She held up a long stick with a mustache attached to the end and waved it in front of her face. "I can't stand that sticky mustache tape."

Section C was darker and gloomier than the rest of the Wolver Hollow graveyard. Tall trees blocked out the moon, and the shadow of the windmill fell across the old graves.

Parker shone his flashlight along the stones.

110 . . . 111 . . . 112 . . .

"One thirteen," said Parker. His flashlight lit upon the cracked and chipped tombstone that read: BOCKIUS B. BEAUREGARD. 1827–1888. RIP. "There he is."

"Told you," Samantha von Oppelstein said.

"Told us what?" asked Parker.

"That there was no mustache," she said. "The only thing I see is some old dead dude's tombstone and two wannabe ghost hunters."

"Detectives," Lucas said. He straightened his badge.

"Whatever," said Samantha von Oppelstein. "Are we done here? Are you convinced?"

"No," Parker said.

"No?" said Samantha von Oppelstein.

"Maybe it only comes out at midnight," Parker said.

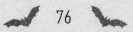

"Parker, we can't wait until midnight!" Lucas said. "There's a curfew!"

"We're already out past curfew," Parker said.

"Your mom will figure out that we're not in your room!" Lucas said.

"Or maybe there is no mustache," Samantha von Oppelstein said. "Just an old superstition."

The crickets stopped chirping.

"Parker?" Lucas asked.

Parker's flashlight flickered and went out.

"Lucas?" Parker said.

"If you're trying to scare us, Parker, it's not working," Samantha von Oppelstein said.

"Stupid flashlight," said Parker. He smacked his flashlight in the hope that he could get it to turn on.

Clouds passed before the moon again, and

everything went dark. They could hardly see their own hands in front of their faces.

"What's that?" Samantha von Oppelstein asked.

"What's what?" Parker asked.

"Something moved," she said.

"Lucas, was that you?" asked Parker.

"I didn't move," said Lucas.

A violent crack of lightning struck a twisted old cypress tree about twenty feet from them, and lit up the entire graveyard.

Parker tried to speak, but the words refused to form in his throat.

Lucas's eyes widened, and his face paled.

Samantha von Oppelstein slowly turned to look over her shoulder.

The haunted mustache hovered a few feet

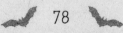

off the ground, caked with crumbling grave dirt and glowing with a pale blue light.

Samantha von Oppelstein grabbed both Parker's and Lucas's wrists.

The mustache started to drift toward them.

That's when Lucas screamed.

That's when Parker's mustache peeled off and fell to the grass.

That's when the mustache lunged.

And that's when the three of them turned tail and ran.

6

"Follow me!" Samantha von Oppelstein
screamed. She did not bother to wait and see if
the boys listened. But Parker and Lucas didn't
need to think twice about it. They darted after
her, and the mustache chased after them.

They ran. They ran as fast as they possi-
bly could, not daring to look back. One mis-
step and they might trip and fall, and the last
thing they would see would be the mustache

from beyond the grave smothering their face.

The clouds raced across the sky, and the heavens trembled with booming thunder and peals of lightning.

Samantha von Oppelstein stopped in front of a small stone crypt with narrow iron doors.

"What are you doing?" Parker asked. "We have to run!"

"It'll catch us," she said, tugging on the chain around her neck.

"These things are locked!" said Lucas.

"Key," said Samantha von Oppelstein. She held up the necklace. A single key was tied to the end of it. She slipped the key into the keyhole and twisted. The door unlocked with a heavy thunk, and she and Parker pulled the doors open.

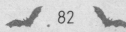

"Hurry, hurry, HURRY!" shouted Lucas. He shoved Parker and Samantha von Oppelstein and fell in behind them. Parker yanked the doors shut just as the mustache reached the crypt, and Samantha von Oppelstein twisted the lock back into place.

It was pitch-black and damp. The crypt had no windows. The dead didn't need light. Nobody said anything for a few minutes; they just listened. At first there was nothing, just the sound of their own labored breathing. Something scurried across the stone floor, and Lucas and Parker stumbled back into each other with muffled shrieks.

Then they heard it. Something tap, tap, tapping at the door.

Tap. Tap. Tap.

Tap. Tap. Tap.

It went on like that for what seemed like an eternity while the three of them huddled in the darkness.

"Does anyone have a working flashlight?" Parker asked.

Both Samantha von Oppelstein and Lucas said no. They'd dropped theirs when the mustache first appeared.

Tap. Tap. Tap.

"Believe me now?" Parker whispered.

"Is this really the time to say 'I told you

so'?" Samantha von Oppelstein asked.

"Will you two cut it out?" Lucas asked.

Something heavy banged against the door, and all three of them screamed and jumped together.

Another bang, and another.

The iron doors rattled on their hinges.

The banging became a hammering, and the very crypt seemed ready to cave inward.

And then . . . it stopped.

Just like that, it stopped.

They listened in silence, waiting for that awful banging to continue. The only sound that came was that of their own rapid breathing and whatever was scurrying around the floor of the crypt.

"Rats," Samantha von Oppelstein said.

"Rats?" asked Lucas. His voice became three pitches higher.

"On the floor," she said.

"How do you know?"

"And how did you have a key to this crypt?" Parker asked. He shook something off his foot that squeaked and skittered to the corner.

"My great-great-great-grandfather is in here," she said. "I come here a lot to——"

"Write poetry," Parker finished.

"Think," she said. "I like to talk to him."

"Guys, I . . . I think it's gone," Lucas said. "Listen." No banging, no tapping. Just the three of them and the rats.

"Now what?" asked Samantha.

"We wait," Parker said. "We just wait until dawn, and it'll be gone. We can stay in here and avoid having our lips eaten, and tomorrow we can tell everyone that we saw it."

"No way," said Lucas. "No way, no way, no how. I am *not* spending the next who-knows-how-many hours stuck in here, in the dark, with Samantha's dead great-great-great-grandfather and a swarm of rats. I can't stand rats."

"So you'd rather have your face eaten by that ghost mustache?" Parker asked.

"Maybe my great-great-great-grandfather doesn't want to spend the next few hours with *you*, Lucas," Samantha von Oppelstein said.

"And besides," said Lucas, "if we don't get that mustache to Hill Crest Manor, it'll just come back next year, and I don't want to spend every October 19 afraid that a haunted mustache is going to come looking for me while I sleep. You saw that thing. I'm going to have nightmares!"

"He has a point," said Samantha von Oppelstein. "Restless spirits have long memories. It might come looking for us. That's what the book said, anyway."

"We have the Handsome Hank's," Lucas continued. "We have the salt, and we certainly have the mustache. . . . Now we need to do what we came here to do."

"Okay," Parker said. "We'll do this."

"Are you sure?" Samantha von Oppelstein asked.

"Yes," said Parker.

"Are you sure you're sure?"

"Yes!"

"Okay," she said. "Here we go. . . ."

Samantha von Oppelstein undid the latch and pushed one of the doors open just a few inches. A cool, crisp October breeze swept into the crypt.

"Crickets," Lucas whispered. "The crickets are chirping again."

Samantha von Oppelstein pushed the door open a bit more.

"See anything?" Parker asked.

"I think it's safe," she said.

Lucas, Parker, and Samantha von Oppelstein peered out of the open doorway. They half suspected that at any moment the haunted mustache was going to drop from the sky and eat their faces.

Nothing happened.

Samantha von Oppelstein stepped out first.

She spun this way and that, waiting for an attack. Then came Parker, and finally, Lucas.

"Where do you think it went?" Samantha von Oppelstein asked.

"Probably got tired of waiting and went looking for an easier victim," Parker said.

"Parker, your mustache," said Lucas.

Parker's fingers found the empty spot above his lip. "I forgot! It fell off back by Bockius's grave."

"Well, it doesn't matter now, right?" said Samantha von Oppelstein. "We *want* the mustache to follow us. We need to lure it to Hill Crest Manor. Between your lip and that tin of Handsome Hank's, we'll be sure to get its attention."

"Come on," said Lucas. "Let's get our bikes."

7

They scrambled over the wall and back
to the sign where they'd left their bikes, where
Samantha von Oppelstein had stepped out
of the woods and scared them. Only this
time, the thought that the haunted mustache might jump out had them on edge.
The tops of the trees swayed in the wind.
The rain wasn't far off.

They walked down the centerline of the

road, three across. Parker and Lucas walked their bikes while Samantha von Oppelstein tossed the container of salt up into the air and caught it. The north road rarely ever had traffic on it, especially not at night, and especially *especially* not on this night, when the curfew was in effect.

"How can we be sure that it'll find us?" Lucas asked. "Do you think it can leave the graveyard?"

"Now that it has targeted us, it'll be easier for it to find us," said Samantha von Oppelstein.

"See?" said Lucas. "This is exactly why we can't wait until next year. I'll just be waiting all year for it to return and come after us."

"The book really said that?" Parker asked. "That it can find us once it's haunted us?"

"Yep," she said. "What would you two do without me?" She stopped throwing the salt and held her mustache up in front of her lip. "And besides, you have the Handsome Hank's. It's going to smell that from a mile away."

They soon found themselves on the edge of town, and still there was no sign of the haunted mustache. They turned the corner at the Wild Hunt Pub and Restaurant and walked down the middle of First Street. The dirt driveway to Hill Crest Manor was at the end of First Street, closed off from vehicle traffic with a rusted chain.

Samantha von Oppelstein pointed the salt container at a streetlight halfway down.

"I think you should stand there, Parker," she said. "With the Handsome Hank's open."

"Then what?" Parker asked. He did not like this idea.

"Then, when it appears, you jump on your bike and ride for the manor," she said.

"And we'll be right with you," said Lucas. "If we were able to outrun it in the graveyard, there's no way that mustache can catch us on our bikes."

Parker reluctantly agreed, and he soon found himself standing under the streetlight. His bike rested against the pole, and he held the open tin of Handsome Hank's mustache wax in front of him.

Ten minutes passed.

"How long do I have to wait here?" Parker whispered.

Lucas and Samantha von Oppelstein waited just out of sight, across the street.

"Until the mustache shows up," said Lucas.

"Try whistling," said Samantha von Oppelstein.

"I'm not whistling!" Parker said.

"You have to draw attention to yourself!" said Samantha von Oppelstein. "Just whistle!"

"I can't whistle!" said Parker. "Okay?"

"You can't whistle?" Samantha von Oppelstein asked. "I thought everyone could whistle."

"Well, I can't!" said Parker. "I'd like to see one of you stand here, holding—"

"Parker, Samantha, look!" said Lucas.

The haunted mustache drifted out of the darkness and floated there, in the middle of the street, shimmering with a ghostly blue light. It was now blocking Parker's path to the Hill Crest Manor road.

"Guys?" Parker said, slowly standing his bike up.

"There goes that plan," Samantha von Oppelstein said.

The mustache lifted the ends of its dirty old whiskers and tested the air, like a snake does with its tongue. It smelled the Hand-some Hank's and locked on to the boy hold-

ing it! The boy with the bare lip! It had its prey in sight.

The mustache charged forward like a raging bull.

Parker screamed and leapt onto his bike.

"This way!" shouted Lucas. He jumped the curb and pedaled down the street, with Samantha von Oppelstein sitting on his handlebars.

Parker shoved the tin into his pocket and clamped both hands on the grips, leaned over

the handlebars, and propelled himself forward as fast as possible.

"The bridge!" Samantha von Oppelstein yelled. "Ghosts can't cross running water!"

"Are you sure?" Parker asked. "How do you know?"

"I read it in *Lester's Lore and Legends*!" she said.

"I hope you're right," Lucas said.

"Me too," she said.

"That's not comforting," said Lucas.

The two bikes raced through town as the first drops of rain began to pelt them. Distant bolts of lightning cut across the night sky, and the crack of thunder rattled windows in shop fronts and homes.

Still, the mustache chased after them.

They passed under Mayor Stine's curfew banner and past the angry eyes of the Wolver Hollow Public Library. When they reached the small town square, and the bronze statue of the town's founder, Francois Gildebrand Soufflé, Lucas cut a hard left. He jumped the curb and pushed through the wet grass.

"Faster!" Samantha von Oppelstein hollered. "The bridge is just ahead!" The dull, red covered bridge loomed ahead of them. Parker glanced back over his shoulder. The haunted mustache was only a few feet behind him!

"We're not going to make it!" he screamed.

"We're going to make it!" Lucas hollered back.

The covered bridge over Wolf Creek was long and dark and high above the water. The only light came from the streetlights at either end of it.

Their bike tires hit the warped boards with a *thump, thump, thump, thump*.

"We made it!" Samantha von Oppelstein shouted.

Lucas skidded to a stop halfway down the bridge, and Parker nearly crashed into the wall in his desperate attempt to escape the mustache.

But Samantha von Oppelstein had been right. The mustache could not cross running water. It stopped just at the end of the bridge. Even though it didn't have eyes, Parker could feel it watching him.

Samantha von Oppelstein hopped down from Lucas's handlebars. Her combat boots landed on the warped boards with a hollow thud. Lucas flipped his kickstand down, and Parker closed his eyes and counted to three. Any second, the haunted mustache would race across the bridge, smother their faces, and latch on to them like some face-hugging parasite.

But the haunted mustache still did not

follow them. The rain was light but steady. It pattered atop the covered bridge. Lucas let out a big sigh of relief.

"I couldn't pedal anymore," he said.

"See?" Samantha von Oppelstein said. "Told you ghosts can't cross running water."

Parker just nodded. He needed to get his breath back. He'd never pedaled so fast in his life.

"The only problem is that we're cut off," Lucas said. "The only other way to Hill Crest Manor is through the woods, and the trail is on that"—he pointed toward the mustache—"side of the creek."

Parker stretched his hands upward, trying to shake off the cramp that was forming. He did not take his eyes off the mustache. "Robby Dugan told me his brother and his friends were building a footbridge just north of the mill. Said they use it for fishing. I'll bet we could cross there."

"But our bikes?" Lucas asked.

"We'll have to leave them at the creek side," Parker said. "I don't think we can cross the creek with them. We'll have to go by foot." Parker held up the tin of Handsome Hank's. "Get a good whiff," he said to the mustache.

It leapt forward but stopped, as if it had banged into an invisible wall. No matter how badly it wanted that mustache wax, and the lip of the boy holding that can, it could not cross that water.

"What are you doing?" Lucas asked.

"Just making sure," Parker said. "Come and get it, mustache." He shook the tin of Handsome Hank's at the haunted mustache.

"Parker, no!" Samantha von Oppelstein said.

"What?" Parker asked. "Like you said, ghosts can't cross running water. See?"

He pointed back at the mustache, which had suddenly drifted a foot inside the bridge, tapping the boards with the ends of its filthy whiskers.

"Unless invited!" said Samantha von Oppelstein. "Which you just did!"

Thump. Thump. Thump.

"What?" asked Parker. "All I said was . . . Oh." He slapped his forehead. "'Come and get it.'"

Thump . . . thump . . . thump. Thump. Thump.

Lucas hopped on his bike, and Samantha von Oppelstein slid back onto the handlebars.

"Hurry!" Lucas said. He pedaled down the remainder of the dark bridge with Parker on his own bike right next to him.

 105

Thumpthumpthumpthumpthump went the mustache. It ran after them, using the ends of its coarse hair like pointed insect legs.

They shot out of the covered bridge, and Parker cut right.

"We'll lose it in the junkyard!" he said.

"If we make it there!" said Lucas. He wiped the rain out of his eyes.

"We're going to die!" Samantha von Oppelstein screamed.

Lucas skidded around the corner, cutting between the train yard and the baseball field.

The mustache reached the end of the bridge and leapt into the air, flying after them. It swatted at them with its left curl, then its right, trying to grab Parker off of his bike. Something both slimy and bristly brushed across the back of his neck.

"Faster!" Parker shouted. "Faster, it's almost got us!"

"I can't go any faster!" Lucas yelled.

They splashed through puddles and kicked up stones and raced along the tall wooden fence of the town junkyard. Parker turned onto the muddy dirt-and-gravel entrance to the junkyard and stopped at the chain-link gate. Lucas pulled up behind him, nearly dumping Samantha von Oppelstein face-first onto the ground. She caught herself on the fence just in time.

"Go, go, go," Parker said, ditching his bike.

The gate was chained and padlocked, but there was just enough room for them to squeeze through. Samantha von Oppelstein hurried through first, then Parker, and finally Lucas. Parker and Lucas backpedaled, falling over each other, stumbling away from the mustache. Samantha von Oppelstein stepped forward and poured a line of salt between them and the front gate.

When the mustache reached it . . . it stopped.

It floated there, studying the salt, studying the chain-link entrance, and watching the kids. It reached out and shook the chains that held the two gates from opening. It rattled them hard enough to shake the entire front fence section.

The stench of the haunted mustache was enough to make them sick. It was a powerful, pungent smell of death. It was so bad that it wafted right over the gross smell of the garbage in the junkyard.

"It can't pass through!" Lucas said. He pinched his nose shut.

"The salt," Samantha von Oppelstein said. She gagged.

"Good thinking!" said Parker. He also squeezed his nostrils closed.

And then the mustache moved to one side. It slipped the end of one whiskery curl through the chain-link gate and began to undo the bolts that held the whole hinge together.

Parker, Lucas, and Samantha von Oppelstein stepped away from the gate.

"Guys?" Samantha von Oppelstein said. "I hope you have a new plan."

"I'm fresh out of plans," said Parker.

"And I think we're fresh out of luck," said Lucas.

The nut turned loose and then fell to the

ground. The washer and bolt followed, and the entire front gate sagged slightly. Three more bolts, and the whole thing would fall in on one side, breaking the line of salt that kept the mustache out of the junkyard.

It floated down and wrapped one curl around a stick, holding it like a pencil. The kids watched in shock as it scratched something in the dirt.

Your lip is mine.

And then it added a smiley face.

When it was done, it dropped the stick and began to loosen the next bolt.

Parker grabbed Lucas and Samantha

von Oppelstein and pulled them with him as the second bolt hit the dirt. The gate groaned and hung slightly askew. Two more bolts, and it would fall inward. And then the haunted mustache could float right inside.

"Let's try and lose it in all of this junk!" Parker said.

They jogged deeper into the junkyard.

The place was a towering collection of old, broken things, abandoned appliances, scrap metal, and ripped-up furniture balanced very dangerously on either side of them. They splashed through the deep puddles without even thinking about it. The only thing they were thinking of was getting away from that mustache.

"Gross," said Lucas, dry-heaving. "I think I'm going to puke."

"Doesn't smell worse than that mustache!" Parker said.

The whole place stank like rotten meat, old vegetables, and moldy scraps of who knows what. But Parker was right, the mustache smelled even worse.

Beady eyes watched them from the dark

corners, and thick, pink rat tails slipped out of sight as the kids passed.

"Why are there so many rats in this town?" Lucas groaned.

"There's got to be a back way out of here, right?" Parker asked. "Like a loose board, or a hole in the fence or something?"

"And what if there isn't?" asked Samantha von Oppelstein.

"Then I guess it was nice knowing you," said Parker.

The front gate crashed to the ground.

"This way," Samantha von Oppelstein said. She pulled Parker and Lucas to the left.

The mustache drifted between the piles of garbage and turned left.

"Hurry up," Parker said. "It's coming!"

"Right or left?" she asked.

"Right!" said Lucas.

They hurried to the right, and the mustache turned after them.

They found themselves in the back corner of the junkyard. On one side, the tall, wooden fence. On the other side, a mountain of garbage. There was no hole, no loose board, no way to climb the fence.

And the mustache knew it.

It floated toward them, dragging that stick along scraps of metal in a slow, deliberate *tap tap tap*.

Parker, Lucas, and Samantha von Oppelstein backed up until they could not back up anymore. They stood together, pressed up against an old, rusted car. The trunk was open,

filled with puddles of oily rainwater and scattering cockroaches.

Parker looked at the open trunk door.

"When I say 'duck,'" he whispered, "dive for the ground."

Parker reached into his pocket and pulled out the tin of Handsome Hank's mustache wax. He popped the lid off, dug into the paste with two fingers, and smeared it across his front lip.

"Two-for-one special!" he said. He positioned himself directly in front of the open trunk. He pointed to his lip and stuck out his tongue.

The haunted mustache dropped the stick and threw itself at Parker's face.

"DUCK!" he screamed.

Parker, Lucas, and Samantha von Oppelstein dove to the dirt, and the mustache passed over their heads and into the open car trunk. Parker leapt up and slammed the hatch closed before the mustache could fly back out.

"Will that work?" Lucas asked.

"Well, it couldn't get through the crypt door in the graveyard, right?" Parker asked. "So my guess is that it can't pass through solid things."

"Now what?" said Samantha von Oppelstein.

"Now we go to the police," said Parker. "Or Mr. Noffler."

"And tell them what?" asked Lucas. "That we have a haunted mustache trapped in a trunk in the junkyard?"

"Yeah?" said Parker.

"When we're breaking curfew and running around town?" said Samantha von Oppelstein. "That'll go over well."

"We've got to tell someone," Parker said. "We have to get that mustache to Hill Crest Manor before sunrise and put this ghost to rest once and for all!"

Frantic thumps and bangs and hammering sounded from inside the trunk as the mustache tried to force its way out.

"Let's figure it out on the move, okay?" Lucas said. "I don't think standing around here discussing it is the smartest thing to do."

They picked up their pace and hurried toward the front gate. They'd just reached their bikes when a car horn blared from behind them.

BEEEEEEEEEEEEEEEEPP!

They froze and then, ever so slowly, turned around. Headlights flicked on, nearly blinding them. The low growl of the rusted car's engine revved and roared like an angry beast.

It was ready to race toward them, and the haunted mustache was in the driver's seat.

10

They scrambled for their bikes as the
engine roared. The old car lurched forward.
Tires sprayed up mud and gravel as the car
fishtailed down the road toward them.

Parker and Lucas, with Samantha von
Oppelstein on the handlebars, tore back down
Granite Street, away from the junkyard.

The old car burst out through the open gate
and screeched a hard right. Two hubcaps went

clattering off. The boys jumped curbs and cut corners and pumped their legs like madmen, desperate to outrun the clattering old car. The headlights kept on them, holding them like flies in a spider's web.

BEEEEEEEEEEEEEEEEP!

The mustache laid on the horn. It swerved left and right, keeping on the kids' trail. "We've got to make the woods!" Parker said.

They reached the mill and turned onto the covered bridge. They biked back through the shadows. Their tires slapped along the bouncing floorboards of the bridge, echoing across the long, dark tunnel.

They emerged from the other end, just as the junkyard car's tires squealed around the corner and the old car sped toward them.

Parker reached the trail first and dropped down the embankment, bouncing over roots and rocks. Lucas was next. "Hold on!" he said to Samantha von Oppelstein.

She gripped the handlebars tight and closed her eyes.

Lucas had just dropped down the trail when the car passed under the streetlight and skidded to a stop.

The old car backed up and turned toward the forest. It shone its headlights on the wall of pine trees that had already swallowed the kids.

The thought of riding through those woods at night would normally have been terrifying enough to stop them. The woods were dark, and spooky, and it was rumored that all sorts of creatures lurked within, just waiting to make a meal out of children foolish enough to enter at night. But these thoughts did not cross their minds. Not when they had a haunted mustache on their tail that would not stop until it had Parker's lip and the Handsome Hank's mustache wax he carried in his pocket. They rode through the woods as fast as they could, up and down bumps and over fallen branches. The trees were so thick that the moonlight barely cut through. There were twisted roots and half-buried stones everywhere, and branches smacked them in the face more than once. It was not an easy ride, and Samantha von Oppelstein's teeth rattled as she held on for dear life.

They emerged from the forest trail and slid to a stop so that they could catch their breath. One end of the trail led down to town, and the

other branch led up to the old Hill Crest Manor. Gnarly trees, scrubland brush and bushes, and tall brown grass stretched in both directions.

"There it is," said Samantha von Oppelstein. She slid off Lucas's handlebars.

The cold, lonely shell of the old manor rose out of the grass off to their right. The brick wall that marked the boundary of the estate was covered in creeping vines and ivy. A twisted, spiked metal fence marked the entranceway to the old haunt. Boarded-up windows seemed to call the kids forward.

"Susie Robbins said her cousin spent a night there," Samantha von Oppelstein said. "She never came back out."

"Billy Weeks said he knew a kid who stared at the tower window too long,"

Parker said. "One week later he was blind."

"And you really want to go in there?" Lucas asked.

"We have to, right?" Parker said. "After all of this? It'll just come back for us next year, won't it?"

Samantha von Oppelstein nodded. "That's what it says in *Lester's Lore and Legends*. Ghosts keep grudges. Obviously this one is super angry. If we trap it here in its last living home and make sure the rays of the rising sun shine on it, it'll be put to rest forever."

"And we'll be safe," said Parker.

"And we'll be safe," said Samantha von Oppelstein. "Us and Wolver Hollow."

"I'm still going to have nightmares," Lucas muttered.

A car horn blared out from deep in the woods behind them. From where they stood, they were able to see headlights slowly bouncing along the bumps and twists of the trail.

"It's coming," said Lucas.

They left their bikes against the brick wall and slipped through the sagging gate, one by one. The manor's front yard was a mess of dead grass and briars and piles of decaying leaves. They didn't waste any time as they hurried up the rotting front steps. The crooked house seemed like it was one strong wind away from blowing down.

"What's holding this place together?" Lucas asked. "Termites?"

"I'm beginning to think that about this entire town," Parker said. "I never really real-

ized until tonight that Wolver Hollow is one run-down old place."

"I could have told you that," said Samantha von Oppelstein. She took a deep breath and pushed the front door open. The old hinges creaked and groaned. A breeze blew up from behind them, scattering leaves inside the dusty old foyer.

"Are we going in?" Lucas asked. "Or are we going to just stand out here until the mustache shows up?"

"The doorway is filled with cobwebs," Samantha von Oppelstein said. "I'm not going through that."

"I thought you liked creepy things," said Lucas.

"I have my limits," she said.

127

"Let me see," said Parker. He took his flashlight out of his backpack and used it to clear the webs. "They're just spiders. Beautiful, actually. There."

"At least the flashlight is good for something now," said Samantha von Oppelstein.

"No, wait," Parker said. "That's right! I forgot, I brought spare batteries! But let's get inside first."

Parker stepped through the doorway and into the old house. Samantha von Oppelstein and Lucas followed, and the front door creaked shut behind them.

11

The house smelled stale, like laundry that had been sitting in the hamper too long, and there were spiderwebs everywhere. Something fluttered above them, and the branches of an old tree scratched at the window.

Parker found his batteries and got his flashlight working again. He shone it around the foyer and through the open doors on either side of them. The place was still filled with old furniture, all covered in dusty drop cloths.

A knobby hatstand lurked in one corner, and the fireplace mantel held chipped candelabras.

Something swooped down over their heads, and the three of them screamed and ducked.

"Bats," said Parker. He shone his light up into the rafters of the second floor.

The rain turned from a light and steady drizzle to a heavy downpour, and a huge bolt of lightning brightened the sky.

"It's Bockius," Lucas said.

"The lightning?" Parker asked.

"No, on the wall. Shine your light over there."

Parker aimed his flashlight where Lucas pointed. A large portrait of Bockius Beauregard hung on the wall, halfway up the stairs. He glared down at the kids through his bushy,

black, angry eyebrows.
But what really got
their attention was
the mustache that
covered half of his
face. It was the same
mustache. The same
mustache that had
been chasing them
all night.

And, as if on cue, a car pulled up out front. The headlights shone through the grimy front windows for a second, and then the engine turned off.

"Upstairs," said Samantha von Oppelstein, pushing Lucas toward the steps.

"But the bats," said Lucas.

"But the mustache," Parker said.

"Good point," Lucas said.

Parker led the way up the steep and narrow steps. He shivered as he passed by Bockius's portrait. They'd just reached the second-floor landing when the front door creaked open.

Parker turned his flashlight off, and all three of them crouched, peering down into the foyer.

Ever so slowly, the haunted mustache drifted in through the open doorway. The moon was bright behind it, adding to its ghostly blue glow.

The mustache tested the air, as if it could sniff out the kids.

Parker gulped.

"Which way is east?" Samantha von Oppel-stein whispered.

"That way, I think," Lucas said. He pointed toward the front of the house.

"Are you sure?" she asked.

Lucas thought for a minute. His mom had made a big deal about planting her sunflowers where they got the most light, especially in the morning. She'd planted them on the side of the house, the side facing the park. The front of Hill Crest Manor faced the park too, so . . .

"Yes," he said. "Positive."

"Okay, let's go," said Samantha von Oppelstein. "Quietly. No flashlight."

They crept, as quiet as mice, toward the room at the front of the house. It was at the far end of the upstairs hallway. They were halfway there when a loose board creaked loud enough to send the bats fluttering.

The haunted mustache looked up and then began to ascend the stairs.

"Go!" Samantha von Oppelstein shouted. They rushed down the hallway toward the door at the far end.

Parker reached it first, but when he grabbed the handle and turned, it wouldn't budge.

"Hurry!" Lucas said.

"I'm trying!" said Parker. He shook the knob and turned it and pushed against the door with his shoulder, but it wouldn't move. "It's locked!"

The haunted mustache floated up the narrow stairs. When it reached the landing, it twitched the ends of its crusty, whiskery curls.

Parker pulled out the Handsome Hank's mustache wax and held it up.

"T-take it," he said. "You can have it. All of it! Just leave us alone!"

"Move over," Samantha von Oppelstein hissed. She elbowed Parker out of the way.

The mustache drifted closer.

"There!" Samantha von Oppelstein said. She turned the knob and pushed the door open.

"How?" asked Lucas, stumbling inside.

"Key!" said Samantha von Oppelstein. She held up the key from her great-great-great-grandfather's crypt. "Doesn't take much to jiggle these old locks open."

The haunted mustache surged down the hallway.

Parker dove in after them, and Lucas slammed the door shut.

It was a small room with peeling
wallpaper on three sides and one large window
looking out over the front yard. The kind of
window that was sure to let in lots of sun in
the morning.

Samantha von Oppelstein yanked open the
moth-eaten curtains and let the moonlight
spill into the room. Rain painted the window
with violent, splattering drops.

"That was close," Lucas said.

"Too close," said Parker.

Something banged on the door. Then two bangs. The door shook and the doorknob rattled.

"Did you lock it?" Parker asked.

"Yes, but, like I said, it's an old lock," said Samantha von Oppelstein.

"An old door, too," said Lucas. "Any second now, and that mustache is going to knock the whole thing right off the hinges."

Four furious bangs in a row.

Parker stood with his back to the big window.

"This is the spot," he said. "This is where we trap him! The salt!"

"Got it!" said Samantha von Oppelstein. She poured a semicircle of salt a foot away from Parker. The mustache would not be able to cross it to get to Parker.

BOOM!

The door bulged inward, and one of the hinges snapped.

BOOM!

Parker held his breath.

"Behind the curtain!" Lucas said.

He and Samantha von Oppelstein hid behind the folds of the curtain while Parker stood before the window, holding the open tin of Handsome Hank's mustache wax.

"This is going to work, right?" Parker said. His stomach felt like those bats were flying circles in it.

Before anyone could answer him, the door flew off the hinges and crashed to the floor.

The haunted mustache pulled itself through the open doorway and locked on Parker. Parker stood, trembling.

The mustache twisted its curls and then rocketed toward Parker.

Parker closed his eyes and waited for the mustache to latch on to his lip, but nothing happened. When he opened his eyes, the mustache floated one foot away from him. It had stopped, pressed against an invisible barrier as if it were up against a window. The semicircle of salt had worked again! The mustache could not cross it.

Samantha von Oppelstein ran out from behind the curtain and started dumping salt to close off the circle. She was quick, quicker than the mustache. Before it could move out of the circle, she'd finished pouring.

The mustache darted to the left and could not escape. To the right and found no way out. It spun in circles, not able to go anywhere.

The haunted mustache was trapped.

Lucas tugged the curtain open just a bit wider, making sure that come sunrise, every bit of sun would pour into the room.

Parker let out a huge sigh of relief. Lucas and Samantha von Oppelstein high-fived.

"We did it!" Lucas screamed. "We trapped the haunted mustache!"

"You will never steal another lip," Parker said. He slipped the mustache wax into his pocket. "Or haunt Wolver Hollow ever again!"

"Rest in peace, mustache," said Samantha von Oppelstein. "You're back where you belong."

"It's over," Parker added.

The mustache spun around, watching Parker, Lucas, and Samantha von Oppelstein back out of the room. It floated there, heaving, simmering, staring at their lips but unable to move from the ring of salt. They hurried down the steps and out of the old house, eager to be as far from the haunted mustache as they could. Trapped or not, they didn't want to take any chances. Fortunately, the storm had become a light drizzle, and the lightning and thunder had stopped. They grabbed their bikes and rode the trail down toward town.

They held their breath without realizing it and didn't exhale until they reached Samantha von Oppelstein's house.

"Thanks," Parker said. "For all that legends and lore stuff."

"Yeah," said Lucas. "You were quick with that salt."

Samantha von Oppelstein smiled. "Are you kidding? I wouldn't have missed that for the world!"

"Here you go," said Parker. He reached into his bag and handed Samantha von Oppelstein a Midnight Owl Detective Agency badge. "Now you're official."

"Really?" she said.

"Yeah, you earned it!" said Lucas.

Samantha von Oppelstein pinned the badge to her dress. "Thanks! I'd better get in the house before someone wakes up. Talk to you guys tomorrow!"

The boys waved goodbye and hurried down the street to Parker's house. Parker peeked in the living room window. His mom was still asleep on the couch in front of the glow of the television.

They climbed the trellis, crawled across the porch roof, and slipped back in through Parker's window.

They were in dry pajamas and under their blankets in minutes.

"Do you really think it's over?" Lucas asked.

"I do," said Parker. "The Case of the Haunted Mustache is hereby closed."

He yawned.

Lucas yawned.

They were both snoring a few minutes later.

The mustache floated there in the circle of salt, unable to escape. The sun was just starting to rise. In the next few minutes, the sun would light up the room, and the mustache would be forever returned to the grave. Its whiskers sagged in defeat.

Something scurried out from the corner of the room. Something small and furry. The rat stopped and licked its paws, then rubbed its whiskers. It sniffed the air. The rat dropped to all fours and scampered to the line of salt on the floor. It began to lick and chew on the salt, and after several seconds had passed, it had disturbed enough of the salt that the ring was no longer complete.

The mustache slipped out of its prison. It reached up with the curly ends of its filthy whiskers and pulled the heavy curtains closed before the sun could fill the room.

Then it traced out one word in the salt.

Revenge.

And that, my friends, is exactly
how it happened. But don't worry,
Parker, Lucas, and Samantha von
Oppelstein were okay. The mustache
never did return for them, and
nobody recalled hearing about it or
seeing it in those parts again. Some
say that it moved on, found a new
town to haunt, new lips to seek.
Maybe it moved to a town near
you. Or maybe . . . maybe it's
in your very town right now.
Be wary, friends. For when the moon
is full and the crickets stop chirping,
that old mustache may return, forever
seeking a new lip to call its own.
Maybe even yours.
Be ready.

Acknowledgments

This book would not have come into being if it were not for the great writers' group that I was a part of. Donna Galanti, Erica George, and my awesome wife, Jess Rinker, thank you. I still remember sitting around the table and Donna retelling a historical story about an explosion that happened in the small town of Stockton, New Jersey. Donna uttered one sentence that stuck in my brain and refused to leave: "His mustache was all that remained." And, as writers are apt to do, I followed my imagination, and a story developed. It wasn't this story, not at first. It was a different story, and it took many shapes and sizes as I played around with it.

I'd like to thank the Highlights Foundation.

It was on a retreat at Highlights that the idea for the Night Frights series was born, and this story, *The Haunted Mustache*, was to be the first of the many creepy tales in the series. Highlights is a great place for writers to sit with their story sparks and ruminate. Amazing things can come from time alone with your words and your imagination.

I'd be remiss if I did not thank Keith Strunk, actor, writer, all around modern-day Shakespeare. It was his book on Stockton, New Jersey, that prompted Donna to recount the tale in the first place. And here we are.

A great big thank-you to my superstar agent, Jennifer Soloway. You are a treasure, and I'm beyond fortunate to be represented by you. Thank you for your tireless work, amazing support, and endless enthusiasm. I'm proud to have you in my corner.

Thank you, as always, to my editor at Aladdin, Karen Nagel. You're like a wizard, Karen. Your insight and editorial eye are amazing. You know me, my style, my voice, my strengths and weaknesses, and deftly push, pull, and prod me in the direction that the story needs to go, and when we're done, we have something far greater than I even imagined it could be. Thank you for continuing to give me the opportunity to create.

As always, I want to give a great big thank-you to my talented writing partner, best friend, and awesome wife, Jessica Rinker. You continue to inspire me and encourage me. And thank you for the supercool Wolver Hollow

notebook you made me to keep all of my ideas straight!

Thank you, Mom and Dad, for letting me chase monsters and dragons even when you thought I should have outgrown it. Thank you for all the trips to the library and the bookstore, and the art supplies you made sure I had.

And finally, a shout-out to our children, who admire what we do even though they might not always get it, lol: Shane, Zach, Logan, Ainsley, Sawyer, and Braeden. We love you kids and hope you'll follow your hearts and pursue your passions and dreams.

Thank YOU for reading, and on October 19, when the moon is out and the crickets stop chirping, make sure you aren't caught without your mustache!